# Sofia
## the First

### Princesses
### to the Rescue!

ISBN 978-0-545-84668-4

12 11 10 9 8 7 6 5 4 3 2 1          15 16 17 18 19 20/0

Printed in the U.S.A.                                    40

First Scholastic printing, February 2015

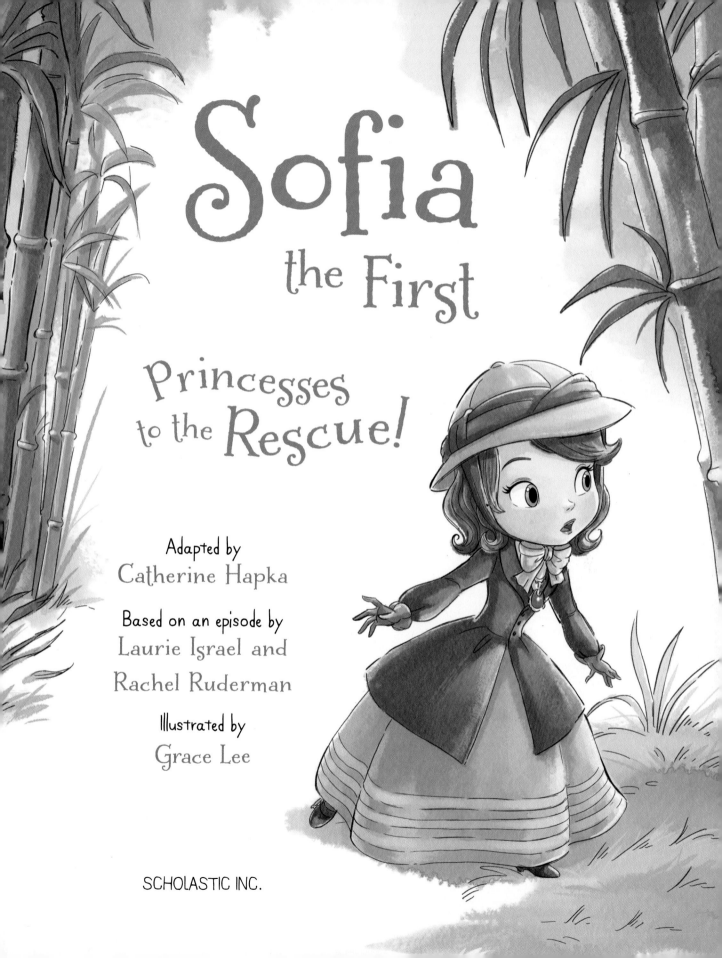

# Sofia
## the First

## Princesses
## to the Rescue!

Adapted by
Catherine Hapka

Based on an episode by
Laurie Israel and
Rachel Ruderman

Illustrated by
Grace Lee

SCHOLASTIC INC.

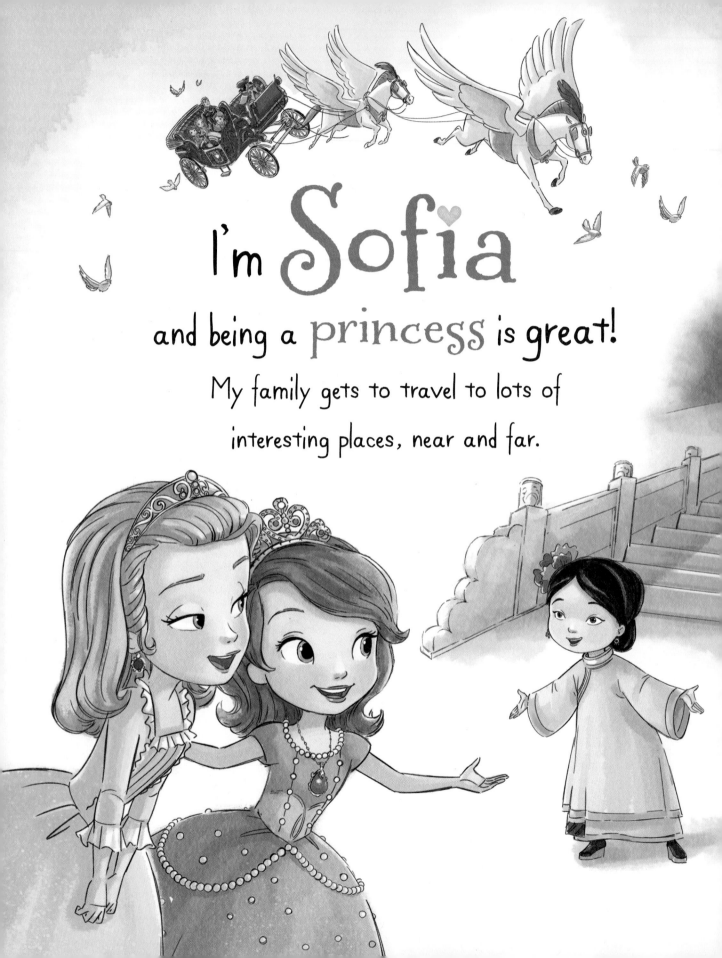

# I'm Sofia

## and being a princess is great!

My family gets to travel to lots of
interesting places, near and far.

Today we're visiting
the amazing kingdom of Wei-Ling.
Our friends Princess Jun and Prince Jin live here.

Soon after we arrive, James and Jin discover
a map to the treasure of the Jade Jaguar.
Before we know it, they're
running off to find it!

When we tell Jin's dad,
Emperor Quon,
where the boys went,
he looks worried.

"A **real** jaguar guards that treasure. We must stop them! Let's go!" he exclaims.

"We want to go with you and help," I say.

But the emperor says it's too dangerous for princesses. Then he and my dad rush off.

I'm pretty worried, especially when the royal sorcerer Wu-Chang tells us about the trap the jaguar set to protect his treasure. Our brothers and fathers could get trapped!

Wu-Chang explains how to find the jaguar's cave.
He even tells us about a secret entrance!
"I will send for the guards to help," he says.
"But you must leave now."

We set out on the path, but soon we see some giant stone statues blocking our way.

Jun spots a sign that says
"The Maze of Warriors." We try to
enter the maze . . . but a stone warrior
moves over and blocks us!

"That statue moved!" Jun exclaims.

Amber nods. "Sofia, this is getting creepy."

"Let's try again," I say. But no matter which way we go, the statues block our path.

Amber and Jun are ready to give up.
"If we can't even make it past statues,
how are we going to get past a jaguar?" says Jun.
Maybe Amber and Jun are right.
Maybe we **should** turn back.

Then I notice my amulet.
It's **glowing!**

We turn around, and
there's Mulan!
"Where do you think you're going?"
she asks us with a smile.
"I never gave up so easily.
And neither should you.
You girls are stronger than
you know."

Mulan helps me climb onto a statue.

I leap to the next statue and the one after that.

Amber and Jun see they can do it, too,

and before we know it . . .

"We made it!" Amber cries.

"See?" Mulan says.

"You girls are stronger than you thought."

"But we still have to save our families," I remind them.

"Can you help us, Mulan?"

"You have what it takes to get past anything
that comes your way," Mulan says.
So we continue along the path, but when I look back,
Mulan is gone.

A little farther down the path,
we hear a buzzing noise.
Suddenly, we're surrounded by silver moths.
There are so many that we can't
see where we're going!

"No way am I letting a bunch of
sparkly bugs mess up my hair," Amber declares,
using her fan to shoo the bugs away.

"Wow, Amber," I say. "That was amazing!" Amber twirls her fan. "Now I'm ready to face that jaguar," she says.

"I'm glad you're feeling braver, Amber," I say. "We need all the help we can get!"

Next the path leads to a lagoon with huge, scary-looking lizards crouching on the shore.

"Lagoon Lizards," Jun explains. "The meanest lizards in all of Wei-Ling!"

Amber tries to shoo the nearest lizard away with her fan, but it takes a **big** bite out of it!

"I **just** remembered something," Jun says, grabbing her flute. "Music calms them down." She begins to play a song.

Like magic,
the Lagoon Lizards stop snapping
their jaws and sway to the music.
I crouch beside one and whisper,
"Mr. Lizard, could you take us across the lagoon?"
"We'd be happy to as long as
she keeps making music,"
the lizard replies.

I call to Amber and Jun.

"Look! These lizards are heading across. Let's hop on!"

It works!

Jun keeps playing music and the lizards carry us
safely across the lagoon.

On the other side, there's a waterfall.
Then I spot something behind the wall of water: the secret
entrance to the cave Wu-Chang told us about!

We crawl through the
narrow tunnel entrance into the cave.

"Look at all the jewels!"
Amber exclaims.

We hear voices, so we follow them,
and we find everyone trapped in a deep pit.

"James! Dad!" I cry.

Dad looks amazed.

"You girls shouldn't be here,"

he says.

Suddenly, the Jade Jaguar leaps out
from behind his treasure!

ROAR!!!

Amber and Jun hide, but it's too late to turn back. We have to save our families. I have an idea! I grab a handful of jewels. . . .

"You want these back?" I say to the jaguar. "Then catch me!"

I scramble back into the narrow tunnel and the jaguar comes after me. "I'm stuck!" he roars.

"That was the plan," I say.

"I need you to let my friends and family go," I tell him.

"After they tried to take my treasure?" he asks.

I nod. "We don't want a single piece of your treasure.
We just want our families back."

The jaguar agrees to let them go,
so I ask Amber and Jun to help me get
him out of the tunnel. Then we find a rope
and help our families climb out of the pit.

Just as we're leaving the cave,
the guards Wu-Chang sent get there.
"You're too late," Amber says proudly.
Emperor Quon laughs. "Yes, the princesses already rescued us!"

Our dads didn't think we could do it, but they are so proud. And that night, there's a beautiful fireworks display—in honor of the three

bravest
rescuers
in the
land!

# The End